Brothers Don't Know Everything

ready, set, read!
BEGINNING READERS

Brothers Don't Know Everything

Linda Lee Maifair

Illustrated by Meredith Johnson

Augsburg
MINNEAPOLIS

BROTHERS DON'T KNOW EVERYTHING

Cover design: Hedstrom Blessing

Library of Congress Cataloging-in-Publication Data

Maifair, Linda Lee.
    Brothers don't know everything / by Linda Lee Maifair :
illustrated by Meredith Johnson.
        p.   cm.
    Summary: After starting a contest to see who can earn more money doing yard work one summer, nine-year-old Christina and her older brother Charlie make some surprising discoveries about responsibility and teamwork.
    ISBN 0-8066-2635-6 (permanent paper) :
    [1. Brothers and sisters—Fiction.   2. Moneymaking projects—Fiction.   3. Contests—Fiction.   4. Responsibility—Fiction.]
    I. Johnson, Meredith, ill.   II. Title.
PZ7.M2772 Br   1993
[Fic]—dc20   93-4605
                                                              CIP
                                                               AC

The paper in this publication meets the minimum requirements of American National Standard for Information Sciences—Permanence of Paper for Printed Library Materials, ANSI Z329.48-1984.   ∞™

Manufactured in the U.S.A.   AF 9-2635

97   96   95   94   93   1   2   3   4   5   6   7   8   9   10

For my sister and brother
who put up with me even when I
thought I knew everything.

Contents

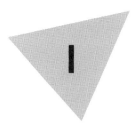

The Bet

"It was *my* idea, Charlie Booker, and you can't use it!"

Christina Marie Booker put her hands on her hips. She glared up at her older brother. She hated it when he gave her one of his I'm-bigger-and-smarter looks. Now that he was going into sixth grade, he gave her that sort of look a lot.

He gave her one now. "You can't do it anyway, Bookworm. You're just a kid." He wrinkled up his nose at her as if she were a wad of slime. "And a *girl*."

She hated it when Charlie called her "Bookworm."

"Prissy Pricilla" Parker had given her that name just because she spent a lot of time reading and got the best grades in their third grade class. Charlie called her "Bookworm" all the time. Except for Mom, Dad, and her best friend Marcie, so did just about everybody else.

"So what?" Christy said. "Girls can cut grass and rake yards just as well as boys. Maybe better. And I'm not a kid! I'm almost ten." She wouldn't be ten until the middle of October—five months away—but she thought it was close enough.

Charlie didn't. He laughed. "You're only nine." He made a face at her again. "And scrawny, too. Nobody would hire you to take care of their lawn. You wouldn't make a cent."

Maybe he's right, Christy thought.

But her dad had said they couldn't afford to send her to church camp this summer. Christy had to come up with a way to earn the money herself.

Cutting the neighborhood lawns had seemed like a good idea an hour ago. Dad hated doing yardwork. Before he got laid off at work, he even paid Charlie five whole dollars to cut the grass every Saturday.

It had seemed like a surefire way to make money. She called up her friend Marcie and asked if she wanted to go into the lawn cutting business. The trouble started when Charlie overheard the conversation. Then he called up his own best friend Billy Marshall and asked him the same thing.

It was her idea, and he had stolen it! It made her mad that he thought she couldn't do it. Christy straightened her back and shoulders, trying not to look so scrawny. She raised her fist under Charlie's nose. "Want to bet?" she said.

Charlie backed up a step or two. "Huh?"

"Want to bet?" Christy repeated. "Want to bet nobody will hire me? Want to bet I can't make more money than you can?"

"Dad won't even let you use the mower, Bookworm," he said.

Christy hadn't thought of that.

"Oh, yes, he will!" she said, not at all sure it was true. Maybe Dad would think she was too young and scrawny, too. She'd worry about that later. Right now she couldn't back down.

"You're just too chicken to bet, Charlie Booker. You're afraid I'll win, that's all."

Charlie's face got red. Christy knew he hated being called "chicken" even more than she hated being called "Bookworm."

"What's the bet, Bookworm?" he said.

She didn't know. "Uh. . . ."

Charlie smiled. "How about whoever loses does the dishes the rest of the summer?" he suggested.

Christy didn't like doing dishes any more than he did. Especially during summer vacation. Taking her turn every other night was bad enough. "Well. . . ."

Charlie gave her another I'm-bigger-and-smarter look. "*Now* who's chicken?" he said. He bent his arms like huge wings and flapped them up and down. "Cluck! Cluck! Cluck! Cluck!"

"Bet," Christy said. She held out her hand.

Charlie looked a little surprised, then took the hand that was offered. They shook, each trying to squeeze the other's hand as hard as possible. Each pretending it didn't hurt at all. Christy wiped her hand on her shorts when Charlie finally let go. Charlie did the same.

"Whoever makes the most money by the end of the month wins, right, Bookworm?"

"Right," Christy said. Her stomach felt sort of queasy, like it did the night before an oral book report. She wondered what she'd gotten herself into.

Charlie ran for the door.

"Where are you going?" Christy called after him.

He turned around and grinned at her, "Billy's dad said we could start with their lawn. That's five dollars already, Bookworm. I can't lose!" He let the screen door slam behind him. Bang!

"Drat!" Christy muttered under her breath. "Drat and double-drat!"

2

Ready for
Business

"I'm sorry, dear. We've already promised the job to your brother." Mrs. Higgins glanced at the old push mower Christy had dragged up her sidewalk. She patted Christy on the shoulder. "Maybe in a year or two, dear. When you're a little older."

Christy had a hard time holding back tears. A year or two would be way too late to win the bet with Charlie. Worse than that, she wouldn't get to go to church camp.

For three years Charlie had been telling her how much fun camp was. Now that she was finally old enough to go, Mom and Dad didn't have the money to send her.

Her hopes of surprising them and raising the money on her own were growing dim. This was the tenth house she and Marcie had tried. Mrs. Higgins was the tenth person to say *no*. Four of them had already hired her brother.

"Thanks anyway," Christy told Mrs. Higgins. She dragged the push mower Marcie's grandfather had loaned them back down the sidewalk. When she reached the street, she pushed it toward Marcie. "It's your turn," she said.

"Why don't we just give up?" Marcie heaved the mower along behind her. "Your brother's right. Nobody's going to hire us."

Christy didn't want to think about her brother being right. She was mad enough at him already. And every time she tugged and heaved at the old push mower she got even madder.

Christy never had a chance to ask Dad if she could borrow his power mower. Charlie had gotten to Dad first. He'd made it sound as if the lawn cutting business was all *his* idea. Dad had even told Charlie how proud he was of him for deciding to work his way to church camp. By the time Christy got home, Charlie and Billy had already finished Billy's yard. They were going from neighbor to neighbor looking for more customers.

"Let's cut across to Meriwood Street," Christy suggested. "Maybe we can beat them there."

"This thing's heavy," Marcie complained, heaving at the old mower again. "I can wait till Christmas for new roller skates. We're just wasting our time."

The mower was heavy, and Meriwood was all the way at the other end of the development. Even people who hadn't hired Charlie said that Christy and Marcie were too little or too young for the job.

Christy was ready to give up herself, but she wasn't willing to admit that to Marcie. She wasn't ready to admit Charlie was right. She couldn't wait till Christmas for camp money she needed in August.

"Let's just try Meriwood. If we don't find somebody who wants us to cut their grass over there, then we'll quit," she told Marcie. "Agreed?"

Marcie sighed, "I still think we're wasting our time." She made a face at the mower. "But I'll go over to Meriwood with you if *you* do the pushing."

Christy pushed. She pushed the old, creaky mower the three blocks to Meriwood Street. She pushed it up and down a half-dozen sidewalks. She pushed it to the very last house on the street.

"Aren't you ready to quit yet?" Marcie asked her. "I'm hungry."

Christy's stomach growled at the thought of dinner. "You promised you wouldn't give up till we tried every house on the street. There's still one left."

Christy pointed to an old-fashioned house with tangled bushes and overgrown flower beds. She smiled at the ankle high grass. "I've never seen a lawn that needs mowing as much as this one does."

Without waiting for Marcie's answer, Christy half-pulled, half-dragged the mower up the cracked walk. She left it at the bottom of the dusty, sagging stairs. She walked across the creaking wooden porch and knocked on the door. No one answered.

"Let's go," Marcie said. "I need to get home. Mom's going to the mall. I want to go with her."

Christy didn't want to give up her one last chance for a customer. She knew it wouldn't be enough to win the bet, but she didn't want to have to tell Charlie that nobody in the whole development would hire her.

"Maybe they didn't hear me," she said. She knocked again, louder.

This time she heard sounds from inside. Something scurrying across the floor, scratching at the door. A thumping noise, getting louder and closer. "Stop that, Misfit, you naughty cat!" somebody said, and the door opened.

Christy stared at the old woman, a knobby old cane in one hand, a bushy-tailed striped cat rubbing against her ankles. "Uh . . . we. . . ."

"Speak up, child," the woman said.

An Answer
to a Prayer

"I'm Christy Booker," Christy said loudly. "And this is my friend Marcie Washington. We live over on Vinewood. We were wondering if we could cut your grass this summer."

The woman smiled brightly. "Why, bless you, child!" she said. "You're an answer to a prayer." She shook her head at the lawn. "It looks pretty bad, doesn't it? Nobody else even asked if I needed any help."

Christy could barely hide her excitement. The woman hadn't said she was too

young or her mower was too old. She hadn't even mentioned Charlie and Billy. And she needed help with her lawn. She even thought they were an answer to her prayer.

"We only charge five dollars a week," Christy said.

The woman's smile faded. "Oh," she said, her face flushed with embarrassment. "I thought you were going to. . . ." She bent down to stroke the cat and shook her head again. "I'm sorry, child. I don't have the five dollars to spare. Sometimes it's all I can do to. . . ." Her face flushed again.

Christy knew what it was like not to have five dollars to spare. She was the only one in her group who didn't have a new swimsuit this year. She was the only one in her Sunday school class who might not go to camp.

"If your father gets called back to work or finds a new job," her mother had said.

She'd looked worried and tired. "It's all we can do to pay the bills, Christy."

"Oh, we weren't going to charge *you*," Christy told the woman. The words were out of her mouth before she knew she was going to say them. Marcie poked her in the ribs. Christy ignored her.

"I couldn't ask you to do it for nothing," the woman said.

Christy ignored Marcie's tug on the back of her shirt. "Oh, it wouldn't be for nothing," she said. "We thought maybe you'd let us use your lawn as a model. It's right here by the main entrance to the development. People would see what a good job we can do."

They did a good job. But it took them more than three hours. The old lawn mower was heavy. The old hedge clippers the woman, Mrs. Drummond, had given them were rusty. Still, Christy thought the hug and the smile Mrs. Drummond gave them was worth the work they'd done to earn them.

Marcie didn't. "Nobody will hire us," she complained on the way home. "Model or no model. Thanks to you, we'll have to do the lawn for nothing all summer. I won't get my skates. You won't win your dumb old bet either."

Christy hadn't thought about the bet. "It doesn't matter," she told Marcie. "You saw how happy Mrs. Drummond was. And she could never afford the five dollars. It'll be a good deed. My Sunday school teacher, Mrs. Mathews, says we should help one another. 'Do to others as you would have them do to you.' Luke 6:31."

Marcie made a face. "Mrs. Mathews doesn't have to mow anybody's lumpy lawn every week with a push mower."

Christy barely got home in time for dinner.

"Cut any lawns today, Bookworm?" Charlie asked her when she passed him the salad.

He'd already announced that he and Billy had seven yards to mow each week. By the end of the month, his share would come to more than sixty dollars. That was almost half the money needed for camp. And it was more than enough to win the bet.

He smeared margarine on a dinner roll and stuffed half of it in his mouth.

"Sure I did," Christy told him. "I have a list of regular customers." In a way it was true. She did have a list, even if there was only one name on it. And she'd promised to mow Mrs. Drummond's lawn every Friday.

Charlie seemed surprised. He swallowed his roll. "How much will you be making?" he asked her.

Christy stared at her plate. It wasn't

the sort of question she could get around without lying. "Nothing!" she said to her spaghetti. "I decided to do it for nothing."

Charlie thought it was very funny.

The Clipper
Snippers

"We're proud of you," Christy's father told her. He made Charlie apologize for giggling.

The next morning, on the way to church, they drove the long way around to the main entrance of the development. Christy's Mom and Dad wanted to see the work Christy and Marcie had done.

"What a lovely sign!" Mrs. Booker told Christy. "Did you girls do that, too?"

Christy stared at the sign. It was propped up in the yard, out near the street where everybody could see it. A circle of

bright red flowers surrounded Christy's telephone number and the words LAWN CARE BY THE CLIPPER-SNIPPERS.

"What do you call your business?" Mrs. Drummond had asked them when they took a lemonade break on her front porch steps. Marcie suggested "The Clippers." Christy suggested "The Snippers."

Mrs. Drummond suggested a compromise. "Sometimes two people who don't agree just have to give a little and work together for things to come out right." So Marcie and Christy decided to become the Clipper-Snippers. But they had never talked about putting up a sign.

"No," Christy said. "I . . . I guess Mrs. Drummond did it. As a surprise. I wasn't really going to put up a sign or anything."

"Clipper-Snippers!" Charlie snorted. "What a dumb name."

His father scowled at him. Charlie stopped laughing. "You girls did all that with that old push mower?" Mr. Booker asked Christy.

"It took a while," Christy told him. Her arms and shoulders still ached. There were blisters on the palms of her hands.

"I'll bet it did," her father said. "From now on, you can use our power mower. I think you can handle it."

"But, Dad!" Charlie protested. "You promised me I could use it! I have a lot of lawns to cut."

Mr. Booker wasn't in the mood to discuss it. "You'll also have to share the mower with your sister. And pay for the gas you use out of the money you earn. Besides, you boys have Billy's mower, too."

"But she'll just break it or something and. . . ."

Mr. Booker scowled again. Charlie decided not to argue. His father pulled the car back out onto the street and headed for church.

"Clipper-Snippers," Charlie said under his breath of Christy. "Nobody will call anybody with a dumb name like that."

After church, Christy walked over to thank Mrs. Drummond for the sign. "It's beautiful," she said.

Mrs. Drummond smiled. "I can make them for all your other customers, too," she said. "If you find me some old boards to paint them on."

Christy didn't want to tell her she was the only customer the Clipper-Snippers had. She ran her hand across Misfit's thick soft fur. The purring cat had curled up in her lap the moment he'd finished the cream she'd brought him.

"My brother, Charlie, says nobody will call. He says the name Clipper-Snippers is dumb."

"Brothers don't know everything," Mrs. Drummond told her.

Christy smiled. She liked Mrs. Drummond more and more.

"You bring me those boards, child. We'll show old Charlie he's not so smart."

5

In Over
His Head

Mrs. Drummond was right. Brothers didn't know everything. Two people called Christy on Monday, asking if the Clipper-Snippers could do their lawn.

Both new customers had looked doubtful when Marcie and Christy showed up with Mr. Booker's mower and grass trimmer and Marcie's grandfather's old wooden rake. But they let them mow their lawns anyway.

The girls were slow and careful. They cut and they trimmed. They raked up the clippings. They swept the walks. They even weeded the flower beds just the way Mrs. Drummond had shown them.

They did such a good job, Mr. Trindel gave them a dollar tip, each. "It's worth seven dollars a week not to have to do it myself," he said. "Especially when you kids do such good work. I'll tell some of my friends."

By the end of the week, the Clipper-Snippers had four paying customers. Mrs. Drummond's CLIPPER-SNIPPER signs were proudly displayed on their neatly mowed lawns.

Christy wasn't the only one getting telephone calls. "Matt Jamison called this afternoon," Mr. Booker told Charlie at dinner. "You were supposed to do his lawn today."

Charlie took a long time swallowing his pizza. They always had pizza when it was Mr. Booker's turn to cook. He just called the Pizza House, and they delivered dinner to the door. Nobody minded. They'd all tasted Mr. Booker's cooking.

"I, uh . . . had a game this afternoon," Charlie said.

"Did you do the Wilson lawn?" Mr. Booker asked. "They had company coming for a cookout. You were supposed to do it by tomorrow."

"Uh . . . no," Charlie admitted. "We're a little behind in our schedule. Six yards is a lot to do, and. . . ."

"I thought you had seven customers," Mr. Booker interrupted. "What happened to the other one?"

Charlie didn't look too eager to tell him. "The Campbells decided they didn't need us," he said.

"The Campbells on Wildwood?" Christy asked him.

Charlie nodded.

"They called and asked if the Clipper-Snippers could do their lawn from now on. They said the boys they had before didn't show up. Mrs. Campbell said. . . ."

Charlie glared at her. The expression on his face warned her to be quiet.

Mr. Booker had heard enough. "Just how far behind are you, Charles?"

Charlie set down his pizza. He'd lost his appetite. It was never a good sign when Dad called them Christina or Charles. "Two or three days . . . that's all," he mumbled.

Mr. Booker scowled. He waited for an explanation.

"Bookworm . . . I mean Christy gets the mower in the morning. And Billy's dad said we couldn't use his anymore because we forgot to put oil in it and ruined. . . ." Charlie decided not to finish that part of the story. He took a drink of his apple juice, stalling for time.

"And?" Mr. Booker asked.

Charlie couldn't stall any more. "And we've got ball practice every night, Dad. And we like to go to the pool in the afternoon. And, well, who wants to spend his whole summer cutting grass anyway?"

"You should have thought of that before you took on the jobs," Mr. Booker told him. "People expect you to be there when you're supposed to be. If the job is too much for you, you'd better tell them to find somebody else."

Mr. Booker smiled at Christy. "I know a couple of girls you could recommend."

The thought of recommending Clipper-Snippers to *his* customers, made Charlie sick.

"We'll get caught up, Dad. Tomorrow. We can do it."

"You'd better," Mr. Booker warned him. "If I get any more complaints, you're out of the lawn care business. And you can forget about church camp. You need to be more responsible, young man." He smiled at Christy again. "Like your sister."

Charlie listened to the rest of Dad's lecture. He promised to try harder. Then he asked to be excused, and went off to call Billy.

Christy ate Charlie's third piece of pizza. She didn't even care if she won the bet any more. With the customers she had, she could make enough money to pay her way to camp. Christy smiled. Her father thought the Clipper-Snippers were good enough to recommend to Charlie's customers. He even said she was responsible. And, like Mrs. Drummond had said, old Charlie wasn't so smart after all.

Christy couldn't remember when pizza had tasted so good.

6

I Want
to Quit

"Why don't you just tell her we're too busy?" Marcie wanted to know. "We have five other lawns to do. Lawns we get *paid* for."

"We wouldn't have so much business if it wasn't for Mrs. Drummond and her signs," Christy reminded her. "I'll do it myself if you're too busy."

Marcie sighed. "I'm not busy, I'm tired. Tired of pushing that lawnmower. Tired of raking yards. I'm dropping out of the Clipper-Snippers, Christy. I thought it would be fun. It isn't. It's hard work. I don't want to do it any more."

Christy thought Marcie was kidding. She was tired, too, but she wasn't ready to quit. Five customers wasn't even enough to win the bet with Charlie.

"We could get the Daltons and the Wangs," she told Marcie. Just that morning, Mrs. Wang had told Christy to tell Charlie his work was sloppy. She wanted him to do her lawn over. "Then I'll have enough for camp, and you can get those new roller skates you've been wanting."

"I'm so sore I can hardly walk," Marcie said. "I may never roller skate again. I don't want to be a Clipper-Snipper any more. And I've got better things to do than sit around all afternoon talking to some old lady and her dumb cat."

Christy didn't argue.

She didn't tell Marcie that she enjoyed Mrs. Drummond's stories. She like listening to her talk about when she was a girl.

Christy didn't try to explain that spending time with Misfit was almost as good as having a cat of her own.

She just got her father's lawnmower and grass trimmer and went over to Meriwood to do Mrs. Drummond's lawn as usual.

As usual, Mrs. Drummond offered her lemonade. This time she'd even baked cookies. . .chocolate nut cookies with thick, fudge icing.

"Where's your friend?" she asked Christy.

"Uh . . . she didn't feel like cutting grass today."

Christy didn't want to tell her that Marcie had quit the Clipper-Snippers. She didn't want to tell her that she might have to quit herself.

She couldn't do all the work herself. Christy had to find somebody to help her. She had six lawns she'd promised to do for the summer.

44

Mrs. Drummond didn't ask any more questions about Marcie. She patted Christy's hand. She understood that something was wrong.

"I hope you'll come see me in the winter," she said. "Even when the grass doesn't need mowing any more. Misfit and I look forward to Fridays now."

Christy decided that even if she only did one lawn the rest of the summer, it would be Mrs. Drummond's. And she'd stop by to see her on the way home from the bus stop a couple times a week, too. She held Misfit close, enjoying the sound of his deep, rumbling purr.

"So do I, Mrs. Drummond," she said.

Mrs. Wang was sweeping her sidewalk when Christy walked by, pushing the mower with one hand. Dad's grass trimmer was slung over her shoulder.

"Look at my yard," Mrs. Wang said angrily. "Have you ever seen such a mess?"

Christy didn't know what to say. The Wangs' yard was a mess. Charlie and Billy had missed whole patches of grass. Long scraggly stubble grew along the walk and around the hedges. The slope by the street hadn't been cut in weeks.

"Did you tell your brother I want him to come back and do my yard again today?" Mrs. Wang swatted at a patch of uncut grass with her broom. "It looks worse this week than it did last week."

Christy shook her head. "I haven't seen him yet, Mrs. Wang. I think he has baseball practice this afternoon. And he has some other lawns to catch up on. And. . . ." She couldn't believe she was defending Charlie.

Mrs. Wang didn't let her finish anyway. "Those boys are always in a hurry to play baseball or go swimming." She waved her broom at Christy's lawnmower. "If your brother doesn't come over tonight, you can have the job yourself." I hear the Snipper-Clippers do good work."

Christy didn't tell her she had the name wrong. She didn't tell her there was only one Clipper-Snipper now either.

She forced a smile. "We're very careful," she said.

If she could do the lawns on her own, and she got Mrs. Wang, she'd have six *paying* customers and so would Charlie.

She wouldn't have to share her earnings with anybody either. She might be able to catch up with him before the month was over and win the bet after all.

Mrs. Wang took another swipe at the grass with her broom. "You tell your brother if he doesn't come over this afternoon, I'm going to speak to his father about this carelessness."

"I'll tell him," Christy promised.

7

Going Out
of Business

It was a hard promise to keep. If Christy didn't warn her brother and Mrs. Wang complained to Dad, Charlie would be out of the lawn cutting business altogether. He wouldn't even be allowed to go to camp. At first Christy thought it would serve him right. Then she decided it would be a mean trick to play, even on Charlie. And an unfair way to win the bet.

"Mrs. Wang wants you to do her lawn over," Christy told her brother. "She's really upset about the way you left it. She's going to call Dad if you don't cut it again."

Charlie groaned. "When?"

"Today," Christy said.

"I can't do her lawn today!" Charlie protested. "I can't get back to her until next week."

"She said the Clipper-Snippers could do it from now on if you don't go back and fix it," Christy told him.

Charlie's smile surprised her. "You want the job, Book . . . Christy?" he asked. "It's yours if you do."

Christy was suspicious. He'd gotten really mad when the Campbells decided to fire him and hire her instead. And he never called her Christy.

"Why don't you want it?" she asked.

Charlie hesitated. "I guess you'll find out sooner or later anyway," he said.

He sighed, deeply. "Billy quit yesterday. He says he's sick of cutting grass and working his summer away. And his dad was really mad about the mower and the neighbors calling to complain."

Charlie sank wearily into a chair. "I'm further behind than I was before, and I'll never get caught up on my own. If it wasn't for camp, I'd quit myself. This is a lot harder than I expected it to be."

He shook his head. "Dad isn't going to like this. You know how he feels about finishing something you started and being responsible."

Christy nodded. She knew exactly how he felt. The lawn cutting business had turned out to be a lot harder than she'd expected too. And she'd gotten the "You have to be more responsible, young lady!" lecture at least a hundred times herself.

"You want the Wangs?" Charlie asked her again. "You can have the Jacobys, too. I can't take care of everybody on my own."

With the Wangs and the Jacobys Christy would be sure to win the bet. But without Marcie, she'd never be able to do the lawns she had now.

"Sometimes two people who don't agree just have to give a little and work together for things to come out right," Mrs. Drummond had told her. It had worked for the Clipper-Snippers. She wondered if it worked for brothers too.

"Neither can I," Christy admitted.

Charlie looked confused. "What?"

"Marcie quit on me, too. This morning. I did Mrs. Drummond's yard on my own. It took forever. I can't take care of everybody on my own either."

Charlie laughed. "Looks like neither one of us will raise the money for camp now. We'll both be out of business pretty soon."

"Maybe not," Christy told him. "All either of us needs is a good partner."

"I don't know anybody else who'd spend half the summer helping me cut grass, do you, Bookworm?"

Christy held out her hand. "If you help me with my lawns. . .and stop calling me Bookworm, I do."

8

A New Team

"I want to play ball," Charlie said. "I've spent the whole week cutting grass. And you don't even get paid for this one."

"You don't get paid for cutting our grass any more," Christy pointed out. "But you still do it."

"That's not the same," Charlie argued. "Dad would pay me if he could. And, well, it's my yard, too. It makes me feel like I'm helping him a little."

"That's why I do Mrs. Drummond's yard," Christy told him. "It makes me feel like I'm helping a little. She'd pay if she could."

Christy thought of the way Mrs. Drummond sat out on her porch waiting for her every Friday. The way she smiled when she saw her coming down the walk. "I think the visit means more to her than the yard work." The visit had come to mean a lot to Christy, too.

"Then why don't we just go over and visit and forget the work?" Charlie asked. His sheepish grin told Christy he didn't really mean it.

"Oh, go to your game," Christy told him. "I'll do it by myself." She started to drag the mower out of the garage. "Even if I *did* help you with our yard last week."

Charlie made a face. "OK, OK. If we do it together I guess it won't take very long."

He handed Christy the grass trimmer and took over the mower. "You know, we're getting pretty good at this grass cutting business."

Charlie was right. He and Christy worked out what Charlie called "a system." Since he was taller and stronger, he pushed the mower. Since Christy was neater and more patient, she did the trimming and sweeping.

When Charlie finished the cutting, he helped her with the raking. They worked side by side with two old rakes they'd bought at a yard sale.

The lawns were done faster and better than before. They hadn't lost another customer. There hadn't been any more complaints either.

Working together, they had Mrs. Drummond's yard done in plenty of time for Charlie to go to his game. He hung around, eating his share of the brownies Mom had sent over.

Mrs. Drummond told a story about the time she and her older brother tried to sneak into the circus. The circus manager had put them to work to pay their way into the show. They got to feed the animals and sweep out the tent. They'd enjoyed every minute of it.

"I gotta go," Charlie said when the story was over. "Josh and Billy will have a fit if I miss another game. Our team's tied for first place." He thanked Mrs. Drummond for the lemonade. "We'll be back next week," he promised.

"You and your sister make quite a team yourselves," Mrs. Drummond told him.

Christy looked up from the cat toy she was dangling in front of Misfit. "You haven't seen the way we argue at home," she told Mrs. Drummond. "Charlie thinks I'm a pest."

Charlie nodded vigorously. "She is a pest," he said. For once, he smiled when he said it.

"Who won the bet?" Mrs. Drummond asked as they watched Charlie push the mower down Meriwood toward home.

Christy hadn't thought about the bet for two weeks. She and Charlie had been making exactly the same amount of money since they became partners. But he'd been ahead of her before that.

"I guess he did," she said.

She'd be doing the dishes every night the rest of the summer. Somehow it didn't matter so much any more. She'd proved she could do the job she set out to do.

By the end of the summer she'd have enough money for church camp and Christmas gifts for Mom, Dad, and Charlie. She'd be sure to save enough to buy a little something for Mrs. Drummond and Misfit too. Maybe Mom would invite them over for Christmas dinner.

Christy got home in time to help Mom fix supper.

"A roast?" she asked. Her mouth watered at the thought of it. The last time they'd had a roast was her father's birthday. Pizza from the Pizza House was the biggest treat they'd had in months.

"Are we celebrating something?" she asked her mother.

Mom smiled brightly. "Your father got that job at Henderson. He starts on Monday."

Christy was so happy about the new job she didn't mind the extra dishes they dirtied baking a chocolate cake with chocolate icing. It was a surprise for her father.

When the meal was over, she helped her mother clear the table and started stacking the dishes in the basin.

"I thought it was Charlie's turn to help," her mother said.

"Uh, yeah, well. . . ." Christy said, not sure how to explain. "We sort of have an arrangement. I'm going to do the dishes for the rest of the summer."

Mom raised an eyebrow in curious surprise. But she didn't ask questions Christy didn't want to answer. She took out a clean dishtowel and started drying the dishes as Christy washed and rinsed them.

Charlie came into the kitchen and took the towel from his mother. "Dad says there's a movie on TV you'd like," he told her. "Christy and I can do these. We're used to working as a team. Aren't we, Bookworm?"

Christy nodded. She was so astonished she didn't even mind him calling her Bookworm.

Looking more curious and surprised than ever, Mrs. Booker went into the living room to watch TV with her husband. Christy heard her father's deep, hearty laughter. It made her feel good. He hadn't laughed much lately.

She washed a vegetable bowl and set it on the drainboard. "You don't have to do this," she told Charlie. "You won the bet. You made more than I did."

Charlie picked up the bowl and wiped it with the towel. He set the still-damp bowl on the cupboard shelf. Then he reached for another dish and grinned at Christy. "Yeah, I know," he said.